English Cream

THE WHISPER CHRONICLES
and
DIVA

RENATE MODEL
Sketches by Laura Orefice Stevens

English Cream
Copyright © 2022 by Renate Model

All rights reserved. No part of this book may be reproduced in any form or by any electronic or mechanical means, including information storage and retrieval systems, without permission in writing from the publisher and author, except by reviewers, who may quote brief passages in a review.

This publication contains the opinions and ideas of its author. It is intended to provide helpful and informative material on the subjects addressed in the publication. The author and publisher specifically disclaim all responsibility for any liability, loss, or risk, personal or otherwise, which is incurred as a consequence, directly or indirectly, of the use and application of any of the contents of this book.

ISBNS:

Paperback 978-1-951901-74-5
Hardback   978-1-951901-73-8
Ebook   978-1-951901-75-2

Printed and bound in The United States of America.

Books by Renate Model

Confessions of a Red Stove
Cat's Cradle
White Ibis Dawn
Tuesday's Child
The Way We Dance Now

Renate Model

IN MEMORY

    Kelly
    Katydid
    Florian
    Tallyrand
    Foxtrot
    Zazie
    Zoe

Asleep in a Bedford fern garden

The Whisper Chronicles

Angels

In the scheme of things, it seems
I am God to three
rascally Dachshunds. My hands
prepare their food, my fingers
groom their tangled fur. Mine
is the law of the leash.

Truth is, I am in awe
of their beauty, their exuberant
response to absolutely all the world,
their simple patience
with my complicated moods,
(Can we go too? Must we stay?)
God decides.

If it's true that I am God,
then these are my angels, angels
who bark too much,
angels who steal butter from
God's table, and, if there are carpets
in heaven, for sure there will be
occasional angel poop.

Renate Model

Renate Model

WHISPER, that's ME. I have the biggest, loudest bark of any of my Lady Mum's Dachsies, 7 before me. They don't bark anymore because they're dead, all except Zazie, and she is almost dead. My Lady Mum says I have a 10 gallon bark because I was born in Texas. Everyone in Texas has a 10 gallon something or other. They bark or drawl. I bark or growl, or pee. My Texas mum, Karen, brought me from Texas to my Lady Mum in New York, So I have 3 mums. How many do you have?

I think I remember my Dachsie Mum. She tasted good. I must have tasted good too because she licked me all over. My Lady Mum doesn't do that but I lick her. She tastes good too, salty.

Texas has weird Dachsies. My Texas Mum, Karen has Dachsies called Borzois. They're tall and skinny with long legs like folding tables. I have short legs but I bet I can run faster than Borzoi Dachsies. I could have been adopted in Texas, maybe by a cowboy, "Get along little doggie," -- I'm a long little doggie. -- I'd maybe live on a ranch and bark at cows. I've never seen a cow. Do they bark? I bet I bark louder. Do they scratch? Cats scratch and meow. Cows don't meow.

Most of the time I don't bark, I am quiet, beautiful and quiet. Serene. That's a nice word, serene. I am a beautiful serene little English Cream mini Dachsie from Texas, with long cream colored fur and short legs and white toe nails and black cherry eyes and a chocolate nose and a big bark. I'm called Whisper. How cool is that?

My Lady Mum talks about lineage." Sounds like something you wash. I think she means laundry. But she says "no, it means standing in line behind you." How do you do that? She says it means first there was Kelly, a mini Dachsie with long hair, red hair. Then Katie, called Kelly's Katiedid, because he adopted her too, another mini with long red hair. She lived to be very old. Next was Florian, a gentle mini Dachsie with long black and tan hair and loved to pieces. He died on a November day. My Lady Mum says Florian was only 7 when he died. I can count to 7. Some photos show smoke trails in the sky that day, made by planes crossing, into a star. My Lady Mum says it was a bandage for her broken heart. I would have licked her nose or nibbled her ear, but I was still in heaven, I think. Think I'll nibble her ear anyway.

Then Talleyrand, snooty, aloof, nose in the air, long long black hair. My Lady Mum says "aristocrat" like his name. The word is longer than he was. He nibbled trouser legs and pillow cases and never even said "sorry." My Lady Mum says he was "high strung" whatever that means. I think he missed someone called Napoleon. I don't think Napoleon was a Dachsie but he had did have short legs.

Talleyrand should have said sorry. Dachsies know how to say sorry They have to. We're really good at that. You tuck your tail under and hang your head and look up so the whites of your eyes show, and whimper a little. I get lots of practise saying I'm sorry, even if I'm not.

Then Foxtrot, beautiful beautiful Foxtrot, a red mini Dachsie. He was the best Dachsie of all, untill me, so beautiful (until me) so loving, (until me.) I almost remember him though he died long before I was born. I think we all played together in Dachsie heaven before we were adopted. Now all the dead Dachsies are sleeping in our Bedford garden, wrapped in ferns and moss, in a special place with a shell fountain for rainwater, but no toys. I wish they had toys. They could play.

Then my Lady Mum adopted Zazie, round as a meatball, black and tan, mini, with very wavy tangled hair. Makes you want to hold her nose in one hand and her tail in the other and pull and pull to make her longer. Dachsies aren't meatballs, though we are called wiener. Zazie never gave up even one ounce of her plumpyness. She was like a daisy, "loves me, loves me not," sometimes let me cuddle with her but mostly nipped my nose if she was in a nippy mood. She was really old. I guess when you are really old you're nippy and forget how to play.

Then Zoe came to live with us when someone asked my Lady Mum to find a home for her. She was tiny tiny, a mini mini with really long red hair. She was already 8 years old when my Lady Mum adopted her and that's old. She lived in my Lady Mum's arms until she died before Papa Wolfe died, which she wasn't supposed to do, but that's what dogs do, leap ahead. She leaped ahead. I guess Papa Wolfe wanted a Dachsie to cuddle. Somewhere there must be ghost Dachsies that are loved and cuddled by ghost Mums and Papa Wolfes.

My Lady Mum just went to the kitchen. gotta go, bye

Two

Now there is ME, Whisper. My Lady Mum says she knew my name before she even saw me. So I was born Whisper. That's cool. I love being Me. I'm very beautiful. I have white toenails. Did I tell you that? White toe nails and lavender eyelashes, well, almost lavender. I'm very serene.

My Lady Mum spoils me. And I spoil her. First thing every morning we have a kiss- cuddle, a sort of love rumble I get nuzzled all over. I get a belly rub. I lick her nose and nibble her fingers and she says "Owowow" and I stop and make I'm sorry eyes. Then I get baby hiccups and she rubs my belly again. Then I stretch, Dachsie yoga.

I have lots of fun names, Kiss-Cuddle, Smooch-Pooch, Pish-Posh, Shnoodle. Barbara, my sky kennel mum, calls me Bergdorf Blond. What's a Bergdorf? Did I tell you I have a sky kennel mum? I mostly come running when my Lady Mum opens Beggin Strips no matter what I'm called. Oh, my sky kennel is up up two floors more up than my New York apartment. I have 2 homes, Bedford and New York, and sometimes sky kennel. So I have 3 homes and 4 moms and 5 beds and lots of chewed up toys.

Three

There's a big box in the hall and I think it has a something in it for me. It's too big to be a toy. I've already chewed the corners of the box but I still can't peek in. I'm a little scared I won't like it. Maybe I'll chew the box some more. I don't think I want what's inside. My Lady Mum says it's for me and it has wheels and when she has to go somewhere I can't go, maybe I could roll around the house in the box, on wheels. I chew another corner. My Lady Mum shoos me away. Grownups!! So I pee.

The box finally got open without me and all sorts of stuff came out. My Lady Mum spent all day, until my dinner time, fussing, putting together what looked like another box but with bars you could see out of, She put one of my beds in the box, I have lots of beds, and some toys, and she put my dinner bowl in the box with some kibble. She said it was like a private Dachsie dining room. I climbed in for the kibble but when I wanted to get out and follow her to the kitchen my Lady Mum put me back in. the box So I peed.

Four

I have 5 beds, 3 smell Dachsie. One of them is really chewed up. I like that one best. I pull stuffing out of it and shake it all over and my Lady Mum scolds and has to crawl around the floor picking up all that fluffy gray stuff, and I pull out some more. That's fun. Two are 2 new ones that smell of me. My really favorite one is in the kitchen and that one has lots of smells. It mostly smells of Zazie. It's really her bed but I'm littler than she is and I jump In first. Sometimes there are kibble crumbs. It doesn't have wheels. Zazie likes to wait in the kitchen bed while my Lady Mum fixes her dinner, so I do that too, in the kitchen bed. We have two bowls, and I want the first one that's put down but Zazie is very fast when it means food. She eats fast too and tries to push her nose into my bowl after she empties hers. That's why she is so round. It's all that kibble in her belly.

What I really really like is pushing my nose into Zazie's bowl when she's eating and hear her yip. She snaps at me too and says I'm pushy. She says that even when I try to curl up with her in her bed like I did with my Dachsie mum. She doesn't always let me. She says I'm pushy. At night I curl up with My Lady Mum, right near her ear and nibble until she says "Owowow." So I nibble the pillow. Zazie doesn't curl up with my Lady Mum. She's too old and fat to jump up. Poor Zazie. I think it's very nice of me to curl up with her in her bed sometimes.

Five

Toilet paper is so fun. I can bite the paper end and run all the way from the bathroom to the kitchen and it unrolls after me and my Lady Mum chases me. I can run faster. She tries to roll it back up and I just run faster and there's shreds of toilet tissue all over the house and she has to stoop down and gather it all up and I watch her and get scolded but not mean scolded, laughing scolded. Do Dachsies laugh? They should because grownups are so funny.

English Cream

I'm getting longer, except when I curl up like a cinnamon bun. Then I'm round like Zazie. She's round like a meatball but when she's not being nippy she's round like a cinnamon bun. My Lady Mum said she wanted to measure me. She got a long stick and told me to stand still, but I was afraid the stick would bite me so I bit It first. Then my Lady Mum got a stringy thing she said is a measuring tape but I said it's a toy so I chewed it. I chewed the stick too until it was just a bunch of toothpicks and It tasted awful so I spit it out and threw up, so my Lady Mum took it away and the measuring tape too. Grownups! So I peed.

Here's what My Lady Mum does. When I nip at Zazie to get her to play with me and she yelps, my Lady Mum throws a shawl over me until I can't see and I have to wriggle my way out from under. Then I nibble the shawl and chew the fringe until my Lady Mum takes it away. The shawl was really my idea. I pulled it out of a drawer in the first place. Grownups are always changing their minds about what is a toy and what isn't?. If you can pull it or chase it or chew it 's a toy, isn't it ? Grownups! So I peed.

Eight

New game! I call it Race Course. I run really fast up and down the hall to the kitchen and back down the hall to the bedroom and back up the hall to the kitchen and back to the bedroom , except in Bedford where I get to run in circles outside until I stop to sniff a mole burrow. Moles don't play, they just dig holes and disappear, Did I tell you I have a house and nice big yard in a place called Bedford?

My lady Mum told me about Kelly, her first mini Dachsie, really her daughter Robin's Dachsie because Robin was invited to go to Spain with a friend or she could adopt a Dachsie. She decided to adopt a Dachsie and not go to Spain. That was smart. I think Dachsies are more fun than Spain. What is a Spain anyway? If it isn't kibble or a bone or a toy, it couldn't be much fun. Don't go to Spain.

Robin adopted Kelly and then she found a special club for Dachsies. There was a race for Dachsies and Robin entered Kelly. He ran so fast in the race that he crossed the finish line way ahead of the other Dachsies. The judges said Kelly must have started early and they would have to run the race over again. This time Kelly finished even wayer ahead of the other Dachsies, so the judges gave Robin a prize, a glass ashtray. Robin marched up to the judges and said "What do you mean giving a child a glass ashtray? I want a silver cup." So they had to give Robin a silver cup. You don't mess with my Robin. Did I tell you Robin is my New Hampshire Mum? She comes all the way from some place called New Hampshire just to kiss and shnoodle me. I don't think Kelly's name was ever put on the silver cup but I could fix that. I could put some tooth marks on the cup though I

English Cream

don't know how to spell Kelly.　I think Kelly would like that.

　　　　I could run a race and get a silver cup. I run really fast up and down the hall to the kitchen and back and even faster outside in Bedford. Maybe I could run in a race they call a Kentucky Derby or Ascot., something like that. English, I think.　They should have a race for Dachsies. Greyhounds are way over rated.　English Cream Dachsies should get to run at Ascot. They're English.

Renate Model

KISSES AND KIBBLE

Whisper is my day
my night

my laughter
my demonic play

Toys litter my life.

I'm missing a shoe,
a sock,
a gardening glove

Whisper will know
where they are.
I'll ask Whisper

Come, Whisper.
No Whisper

I open the Beggin Strips.

English Cream

"Good Doggie"
Whisper runs off with her treat

Still no shoe
No sock
No gardening glove

Renate Model

Grownups pee in a special bowl in the house but they want Dachsies to pee outside. Why? After lots of "mistakes" and scoldings and "sorry eyes." I think I know how to pee outside. I copy Zazie make a "ploshie." My Lady Mum claps her hands and gives me Beggin Strips so I guess I did good, a big accomplishment, my ploshie. I sniff it and am very proud of myself. I don't altogether copy Zazie. who copied Foxie, who was a boy Dachsie and peed lifting his back paw really high, so Zazie lifts her back paw really high and squats at the same time, kind of a lady boy dog. I just squat and that works fine. You could fall over lifting your back paw really high.

Eleven

My Lady Mum and I eat together, sort of. She doesn't like kibble, which is soooo crunchy, Sometimes I leave some in my bowl so she can try it, which is nice of me, but she never does so I eat it. She eats green stuff, rabbit food, and there aren't any leftovers. She likes hot stuff. I like cold, but sometimes My Lady Mum puts warm milk in a coffee cup and sugar. I get to lick the cup. YUM! And sometimes I get to lick a pot and I have to wait til it isn't hot anymore. My Lady Mum could lick the pot while it's hot, but she doesn't. Grownups!

Noodles are oodles of fun. My Lady Mum wraps them around a fork so they hang down and if I'm really fast I can jump up and bite them. Poor Zazie. She can't jump up 'cause she's too fat. I lick my bowl until it shines and then I lick Zazie's bowl until it shines and she licks my bowl which is already shiny. My Lady Mum never licks her bowl. Sometimes she spills her wine and that makes her mad. She could lick up the spill. I sniff it. It doesn't smell like I want to lick it up either, Why doesn't she drink out of a bowl like I do?

Zazie and I help my Lady Mum wash the dishes but she washes them again anyway so they'll taste like soap, I guess.

Twelve

I have a pink leash and a little pink harness. I like them because they are MINE! Sometimes I chew them and they get taken away. I've learned to come when My Lady Mum has them in her hand. I even hold still for a few seconds but sometimes it takes too long. She fusses too much. Sometimes we go to Broadway where there are lots of dogs to bark at. They bark back but mostly I hide between my Lady Mum's legs where it's safe. Some of the dogs don't have tails, poor things. What do they wag? I guess they just waddle. Dachsies waddle too but it's different. We have tails like rudders side to side and we are very long so when we walk the front walks one way and the back end waddles, like a dance, waving our tail like a flag, It's sexy. My Lady Mum calls it my Marilyn Monroe waddle. Marilyn Monroe was a sort of Dachsie in high heels who was in the movies because of her Dachsie waddle. I get lots of attention when we walk on Broadway, people wanting to pet me and asking my name. I love my name, Whisper. Maybe I should change it to Marilyn Monroe.

I see lots of dogs tied up outside the stores. My Lady Mum never ties me up like other dogs. She'says she is afraid some one will steal me. I steal socks and shoes and gloves and cookies from plates sometimes. I NEVER steal dogs. I would bite anyone who tries to steal me, although some of my Lady Mom's friends say they are going to steal me. My Lady Mom says "Steal the swimming pool. Just throw it in the back of your car. Leave Whisper."

Thirteen

Splash! "Whisper! Shame! You've kicked over your water bowl right on Zazie. I know you want to play, butting your swishy tail under her nose. Flirt! but she doesn't want to play and she doesn't want to be splashed. Dogs don't like to be splashed, like it's an insult. Kids get splashed on all the time, puddles, baths, spilled porridge, anything and grownups get splashed every day in a shower-splasher. Not dogs. Look, now I have to mop up. Whisper, let go of that sponge! Look at me. " I make sorry eyes and my Lady Mum says OK and I get kissed.

Renate Model

Fourteen

I have a zillion toys, and a tail. A very long friendly tail. It wags at everybody, even at my other toys. Sometimes I chase it round and round. Then I do something else. So many throw toys, squeak toys, pull toys. chew toys, fuzzy wuzzies. I think people spend more money on toys than anything else, even their toys, or anyway what they play with, so I save them money when I play with their toys. They mostly take them away. Selfish! So I pee.

Fifteen

I was very brave, really really brave. First of all I woke up hungry and I didn't get any breakfast, not one kibble. My tummy rumbled but I didn't whimper or rattle my empty bowl around the kitchen. I just licked and licked it although it was as empty and shiny as a mirror. My Lady Mum had coffee and I think she snuck in a half a bagel. I didn't fuss when she put on my leash even though she fusses too long with the leash. We drove to Dr. Jeff and I didn't cry when she left me, gave them my leash and actually left me there. It was scary.

I must have fallen asleep because when I woke up I felt kind of funny and sort of hurt and my Lady Mum wasn't there. She finally came and we got in the car and home. I peed in her lap but she didn't scold. I still hurt and I didn't get water or breakfast until dinner. I was very good and very brave. I didn't even throw up.

My belly hurts and I can't even lick it. And if I do it tastes funny and itches. Puppies go through so much. You have .to be really really brave.

English Cream

Sixteen

My Lady Mum brushes her teeth with a little brush she keeps in a glass jar in the bathroom. I never get to play with it, and anyway it's too little. I brush my teeth with one of my Lady Mum's hairbrushes. She has lots of them. She likes to brush my fur and sometimes I bite the brush and run off with it. I've chewed up 3. They brush my teeth. Grown ups aren't all that smart.

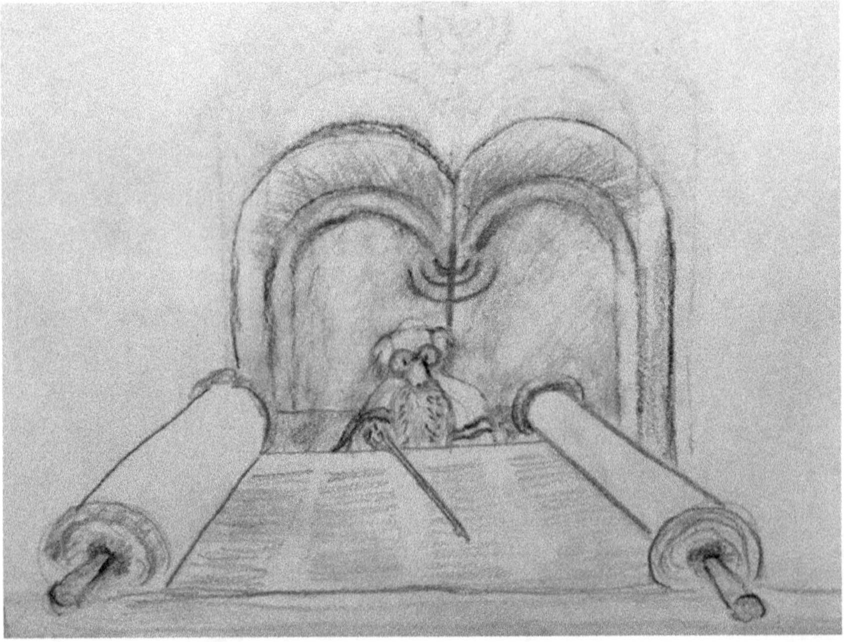

Seventeen

Do Dachsies have Bar Mitzvahs? Or only Jewish Dachsies? Or not even Jewish Dachsies? How do you know you are not a puppy anymore if you don't have a Bar Mitzvah? They tell you at a Bar Mitsvah or you read it in a book called the Torah, I think. Maybe they should have Bark Mitzvahs.

Eighteen

When my Lady Mum says "sit," I stand on my hind legs and do a little dance. I dance when I want to go out, or when I want a treat, or when I want to play. My Lady Mum takes my paws and dances with me. Maybe I could get a little ruff and a peaked hat like in pictures I've seen of circus dogs. Maybe I was a dancing dog in a circus in a former life. Zazie doesn't dance. She just sleeps. She's old.

English Cream

Nineteen

It's confusing. There should be some sort of toy school where you learn what is a toy and what isn't. Sometimes I get a bone to chew on but when I shnuff around outside and find a bone it's taken away and I'm scolded. There are bones that are OK and bones that are not. It's confusing. My Dachsie nose tells me that if it's on the floor or outside, it is mine. That depends on how fast you can grab it, I guess. Grownups!

People toys are weird. Most of them plug into walls. You can't chase them or chew them, except brooms. I like brooms, they play back. Sometimes I go into the hall closet and find toys, coat hangers, rubber boots, mittens, umbrellas. Umbrellas are cool. They have teeth all around that snap shut. I get scared when they open their mouths or snap shut. I think they bite, like sharks. Don't ever stick your nose in an umbrella. They look like they're all folded up asleep but they could snap open and all those teeth. I don't like umbrellas. My Lady Mum isn't afraid of them. She's very brave,

There's lots of other stuff in the hall closet, like old leashes. Sometimes I get scolded for going into the closet but one time my Lady Mum just said "Oh, thank you, Whisper. I was looking for those keys." Grownups!

I like to hide bones under one of my beds, not in the hall closet. Sometimes the vacuum cleaner steals my bones.

English Cream

Twenty

Dachshund Dictionary

Whisper	Me
Little Angel	Me
Little Terrorist	Me
Sit	Stand on hind legs
Down	Jump, up, wait, butt gets pushed down
Stay	Run to Mommy, Whine
Come	Why?
Come !	Maybe
No, Whisper	Meaningless
Bad dog !	Meaningless
Good dog	Wag tail, jump up, yip
Fetch	Get shoe from closet
Let go !	Meaningless
Gently	Only if it's fingers or toes
No barking	Bark
No barking !	(mouth held shut) Wimper
Leash	Jump up, dance, wiggle, turn around
Ploshie	Sniff, sniff some more, pee, (on a rug inside if no one is looking)
Poop	Same as ploshie
Din Din	Sniff your bowl, then beg, make sorry

	eyes
Doggie Bag	A bag that doesn't have a dog in it but
	gets put in the refrigerator when it's
	supposed to be given to me.

Dog House	I've seen them in backyards.
	My Lady Mum's dog house has couches and
	a refrigerator and rugs and toys. It's inside.

Twenty One

Smells are everything. Not so much city smells, where it's mostly schmutz, except for fire hydrants. They smell good.

I like to shnuff in l my Lady Mum's herb garden and smell like lemon thyme, sometimes even lavender. When I shnuff in the compost heap my Lady Mum says "phui" and gives me a bath.

I like to bury my nose in my tail, and other tails. That's the best smell. I like shoes, too. My nose is lavender, Zazie's is pink. I guess that is where we were kissed before the ink dried.

Twenty Two

    The clouds have fallen. All over the ground in big fluffy mounds. And cold! I bit into one and it tingled my tongue. What happened to grass? I jumped and dug and it was cold, but lots of fun. My paws sank right into the clouds. My Lady Mum says snow. I say clouds. Or confetti. Little pieces of cloud fluff falling all over everything. My Lady Mum says there's lots of it in Alaska and dogs run and run all over Alaska in a race called Iditarod. If I can't run in the Kentucky Derby or Ascot maybe I could run in the Iditarod. Someone says "mush" and everybody (if you're a doggy) runs. I think I'll put "Mush" in my dictionary. If anyone says Mush I'll run, even if it isn't Alaska. What is Alaska anyway? Is it baked? I thought it's a dessert. Snow is a nice dessert. It tastes good.

Twenty Three

Christmas, What's that? I think that's when you get Dachsies. My Lady Mum gave her Lady Mum a Dachsie puppy for Christmas one year, in a box with tissue paper and a ribbon. It got all chewed up and the Dachsie peed in the box. And Katydid was a Christmas present for Kelly, but not in a box. There's a tree but if you are a boy Dachsie you aren't allowed to pee on it. Sometimes you have to wear fuzzy antlers or a silly hat. I made a list of stuff I wanted for Christmas but nobody gave it to Santa so I chewed it up along with lots of tissue paper and a plate full of Christmas cookies. So I threw up.

English Cream

Twenty Four

Then you have to make another list for New Year, called resolutions, stuff you promise not to do anymore, or for a year. I worked really hard on my list. Here it is.

English Cream

Renate Model

REVISED NEW YEAR RESOLUTIONS

~~I'll come when I'm called~~
I won't steal slippers or socks or gloves
~~I won't bark more than 10 times at one time~~
I won't spill my water bowl (unless my ball bounces into it)
I won't chew my leash
~~I'll let my Lady Mum clip my nails~~
I won't hide under the bed when my Lady Mum wants
    to clip my nails
I won't spill the waste basket
~~I won't shred tissues when I spill the waste basket.~~
I won't poop on the rug (except where you can't find it)
I won't dig up my Lady Mum's flowers
I won't eat the flowers I dig up
~~I'll be a good Dachsie when I grow up~~

Guess what. It's my birthday just after it's New Year, my first birthday. Maybe I'll work on my birthday list. Maybe I'll just spill my kibble and make sorry eyes and lick my Lady Mum's toes.

Bye now.
Whisper

English Cream

Renate Model

DIVA

English Cream

Renate Model

Diva

Dear Natasha,

Finally, I have the drafts of your new book in my paws. It's gotten so much publicity already I couldn't wait to read it, and now I'm beside myself with envy.. My family will tell you, I suffer terrible jealousy whenever any other dog gets attention. I am an artist, it is just my prima donna nature. I just can't help myself.

Tasha, the book is very, very promising. You will be famous when it comes out, and I certainly hope I will receive an invitation to your press party or book signing. I would come incognito, you would get all the attention. Will your picture be on the book jacket? I'm sure you will look beautiful, the photographers are so skillful. You will be a star in dogdom.

My profile is also beautiful, my nose is very aristocratic. And my coat, burnished copper with sable brushings, like a Titian painting. I'm told I have no unflattering angles. I too really should be in print, "THE MANY LIVES OF KATYDID." Star quality. It would be the kind of book you see offered weeks before Christmas in Barnes and Noble, *and* Rizzoli. "This year's companion book to all the dog books you've ever loved, the flights of fantasy of this little Dachshund will win your heart and the heart of every dog-lover, music-lover, child, artist, anyone lucky enough to receive this beautiful book as a gift, or treat yourself!" That is what the advertisements would say. Part of the text would appear on the dust jacket, along with rave reviews and my picture. Perhaps I could even mentioned your book, "Sister authors, we share a private world of dog-artists, our secret lives played behind closed eyes, under bed covers,, hinted at by wagging tails."

English Cream

The world just doesn't see us as we really are. Wouldn't you agree? It invents Lassie-like roles for us, ignorant of our flights of imagination, our secret achievements.

Almost any evening, lying on my bed, with my family next to me, watching TV, I star in my own world, legs twitching excitedly. My family thinks I am chasing squirrels in my dreams. But that isn't me, the real ME. Some nights the real me is gliding gracefully around a crystal rink in a blaze of spotlights to the strains of Tales of the Vienna Woods, my little legs perfectly executing the most difficult triple Lutz, landing on one miniature skate, my tiny chiffon skirt swirling like a cloud of butterflies suspended on spaghetti-thin rhinestone straps. Then I pirouette with dizzying speed, my chiffon skirt carrying me up like soft white feathers, up over the rink, graceful as a little dove, with lights shining on my fur, iridescent as rubies, and the crowd stands and applauds and shouts "Brava, Katydid," and attendants have to circle the rink twice to gather up all the bouquets of cellophane wrapped flowers from my fans. The judges award me a perfect 10 across the board for technical and artistic achievement. My coach takes me into his arms and strokes my fur and kisses my ears.

That's just a day-dream, although I <u>am</u> multi-talented. My true profession is music, singing, mostly, coloratura roles until now. It's very demanding. I must study all the time, languages, drama, new roles, endless breathing exercises. I am in touch with my deep diaphragm. My voice is evolving, deeper, more resonant. As my flanks darken and the sable brushings become more prominent, I feel a pull toward the richer, more dramatic Verdi heroines. Rossini no longer suits my voice. My voice teacher agrees.

I tell you all this because you mentioned a colleague of mine, Ezio, and quite disparagingly. It's true, he <u>had</u> a beautiful voice, but an awfully inflated ego. Why do so many performing artists have such colossal egos? Ezio's voice was unique, the most beautiful Dachshund tenor vibrato I've ever heard. Too bad he let himself get so fat and self-deluded, imagining himself a Dachshund Pavorotti, calling Pavorotti second-rate. Still, Ezio somehow captured his audiences when he sang, bowing and waving a white handkerchief, until he got so fat he couldn't bow and would only wave. Were you there the night he actually tripped on his handkerchief walking off stage? Quite ridiculous. But that smile, those perfect white canines and pink tongue. The women swooned.

"Encore, encore!" And then it came, Riturno a Sorrento. Always the same stringy mandolins, sounding like a Tour Italy commercial. The crowds loved it!

Ezio's super ego did finally affect his career. But then, my natural shyness and modesty has almost wrecked mine. I'm alright in the ice-rink, surrounded by noisy, adoring fans, but alone, on a vast stage, confronting the most demanding and critical audiences in the world, even though they are always respectfully silent during my piano recitals., It's so, well, confrontational. Ever since that mortifying moment when I actually had to be lifted onto the piano because the stage-hands had forgotten to adjust my bench. I thought I would die. That was in one of my early recitals at Weill Recital Hall. Once I was actually on the keys! I was alright, losing myself in the music, that exquisite concerto for four paws by Liadoff. Shyness is a terrible handicap for a performing artist, the worst kind of stage-fright. My paws go numb and I shiver with the prospect of one more performance.

I'm certainly not alone in this. Glenn gave up concerts altogether and I have, too, except for a master class now and then. My nervous system just can take the strain of a busy concert schedule, different halls, different acoustics, every week. And I need to be so protective of my paws. I can't just run on sidewalks like any other Dachshund. I have to think of my pads, keep them sensitive for the arpeggios. Would you believe, the last time I had my nails clipped I actually had to be sedated? Well, it's true.

So, I've pretty much retired to the recording studio. I'm re-mastering Scarlatti's little known harpsichord pieces for small paws. Do you know the exquisite D.W. 1057 (Dachel Werke)? It's unique in the literature, absolutely pre-figuring the 12-tone scale. RCA claims the exclusive rights to my tapes, on account of their logo, you know, although that dog listening to his master's voice should have been a Dachshund. My lawyer thinks I have a case, thinks the trade-mark may have run out. He wants me to form my own recording company. I don't know. I have no head for business, and it would take an enormous

English Cream

investment. When I think of what has happened to classical music in our time, almost no Dachshunds. Thank goodness none of our breeds is into rock.

I'm considering retirement. I've resisted until now. It's really harder to retire than just to go on. Anyway, no true artist ever retires. First there is the pressure for just one more farewell concert, and of course, there is the money. So many expenses, agents, publicity, voice teachers, language coaches, hair-dressers, costumes! In fact, my voice teacher says I have never sounded better, absolute peak, my voice is richer, more resonant than ever. And my agent is pushing for a farewell concert on the Q.E II, mid-ocean, to mark the end of a two-continent career. What should I do, develop a new Lucia or retire? Such a dilemma. It's enough to send me back to my psychiatrist's couch.

Oh, but that's seductive. I <u>love</u> my psychiatrist's couch, a scuffed-up brown leather affair, not black, thank goodness, too many sexual overtones, and it's sunk in a little, not one of those high, rounded, firm ones so bad for my back. Believe me, it certainly is important to find the right psychiatrist's couch. I tried half a dozen before I got just the right rapport with this scuffed-up sofa and was able to develop the trust so essential to a relationship with your psychiatrist. Now, I relax, stretch out on my back, and am completely confident I won't roll off.

I don't think I get a better hour's sleep anywhere else. We start each session with me talking, free-associating, you know, but also listening until I hear long, deep breaths, a slight snore, then I too close my eyes and snooze.

Uncanny, how he wakes up exactly when the 55 minutes are up. "Katie," he says, "you drifted off. Well, your anxieties seem under control. Shall we schedule for next week?"

Anxieties, my paw! It's a co-dependency with my psychiatrist's scuffy leather sofa, is what it is, a fatal attraction, the leather thing, a perversion. I'm prostituting my art to support this miserable addiction that has me in its grip. There must be a group somewhere, a Dachshunds' Anonymous that will help me free myself, give me back my life.

Renate Model

Meanwhile, the confessions pile up in my psychiatrist's notepad, that is, until he is lulled to sleep by my perfectly trained voice, as completely as any audience when I sing the Willow Song from Otello. Did I mention that I am developing my first Desdemona for Lyric Opera of Chicago, season of 2010? Heavens, I just had a thought. What if my Otello is an overweight Dachshund like Ezio with dog-food breath? Horrors! I guess I do have anxieties. "Same hour next week." I say.

Yours, Katydid

CPSIA information can be obtained
at www.ICGtesting.com
Printed in the USA
BVHW051248020822
643612BV00001B/255

9 781951 901745